T5-AEW-226

Righteous
ROCKERS

Chuck
BERRY

Wayne L. Wilson

PURPLE TOAD
PUBLISHING

Printing   1   2   3   4   5   6   7   8   9

PUBLISHER'S NOTE
This series, Righteous Rockers, covers racism in United States history and how it affected musicians and others. Some of the events told in this series may be disturbing to young readers.

ABOUT THE AUTHOR: Wayne L. Wilson, novelist and screenwriter, has written numerous biographical and historical books for children and young adults. He received a Master of Arts in Education from UCLA. Wilson is a member of the Writer's Guild of America. He is currently at work on his newest novel.

Publisher's Cataloging-in-Publication Data
Wilson, Wayne L.
   Chuck Berry / Written by Wayne Wilson.
      p. cm.
Includes bibliographic references, glossary, and index.
ISBN 9781624694080
1. Berry, Chuck. 1926-2017 — Juvenile literature. 2. Rock and Roll — United States — Biography — Juvenile literature. 3. African American Rock and Roll Musicians — Biography — Juvenile literature. I. Series: Righteous Rockers
 ML420.A45 2019
 784.54
[B]
Library of Congress Control Number: 2018943798
ebook ISBN: 9781624694073

Bo Diddley
by Nicole K. Orr

Chuck Berry
by Wayne L. Wilson

Fats Domino
by Michael DeMocker

Little Richard
by Wayne L. Wilson

Sam Cooke
by Wayne L. Wilson

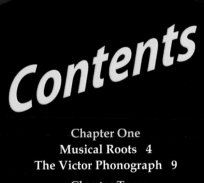

Contents

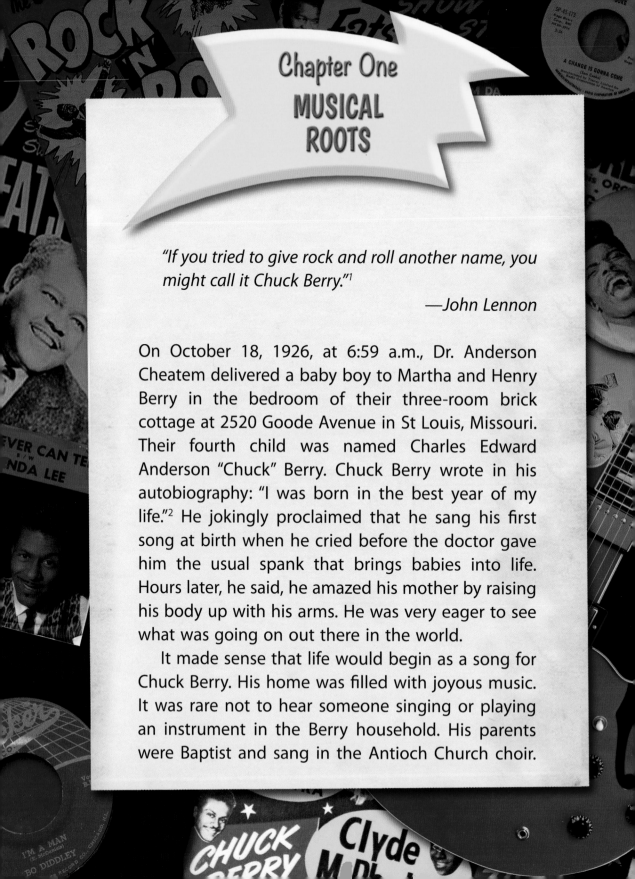

Chapter One
MUSICAL ROOTS

"If you tried to give rock and roll another name, you might call it Chuck Berry."[1]

—John Lennon

On October 18, 1926, at 6:59 a.m., Dr. Anderson Cheatem delivered a baby boy to Martha and Henry Berry in the bedroom of their three-room brick cottage at 2520 Goode Avenue in St Louis, Missouri. Their fourth child was named Charles Edward Anderson "Chuck" Berry. Chuck Berry wrote in his autobiography: "I was born in the best year of my life."[2] He jokingly proclaimed that he sang his first song at birth when he cried before the doctor gave him the usual spank that brings babies into life. Hours later, he said, he amazed his mother by raising his body up with his arms. He was very eager to see what was going on out there in the world.

It made sense that life would begin as a song for Chuck Berry. His home was filled with joyous music. It was rare not to hear someone singing or playing an instrument in the Berry household. His parents were Baptist and sang in the Antioch Church choir.

Rock pioneer Chuck Berry at the height of his fame in 1957. He laid the groundwork for not only the sound of rock and roll, but also the music's showmanship.

The Gateway Arch in St. Louis, Missouri, is the world's tallest arch. It is a 630-foot tall stainless steel monument. Chuck Berry performed in his hometown under the Gateway Arch in 1986.

He loved listening to his mother burst into song in her lovely soprano voice in harmony with his father's booming bass. The Berry family lived only about a block away from the church. The choir often rehearsed their hymns in the Berry family home, gathered around their mother, who played an upright piano in the living room.

Chuck's first memories were of lying in his baby crib and listening to the harmonies of the choir singing Baptist hymns. He would try to crawl out of his crib and into the front room where all that appealing music were coming from. He'd often crawl straight toward the piano. He'd reach up, touch the piano keys, and be amazed by the different sounds he could make. As he put it: "I can imagine the many infantile concerts I attempted at the piano only to be lifted up and carried away, leaving an unfinished symphony."[3]

Even before he learned to walk, Berry tapped his feet to the rocking beats of the Baptist songs led by the rhythmic clapping and stomping of the church deacons. In the Berry home, if one member of the family began singing, another family member would join in and harmonize, no matter what they were doing. Chuck believes most of the words he learned as a child were from listening to his mother sing while doing her housework. The sound of her washboard often carried the tempo of the gospel tunes she sang. He says, "Looking back, I'm sure that my musical roots were planted in me, then and there."[4]

Berry figured he was born curious. By two, he was already asking questions such as, "How did that big wooden cabinet in the front room talk, sing, and make music by itself?" By turning a knob on the box, his parents changed stations. It fascinated him. He'd sit on the floor staring at it, trying to figure out how it worked. His sister, Thelma, told him it was called a Victrola— and the kids in the family were not allowed to touch it.

But Chuck couldn't resist the temptation. One day he got up on a chair and raised the top of the Victrola. He looked down and studied all the parts of the turntable. He placed the needle of the horn to the edge of the record, just like he saw his father do. When he heard the music play, he got so excited he played the same song over and over. His mother caught him playing the forbidden machine and he received his first of many whippings. He would receive many more during his childhood and teenage years.[5]

The Victrola housed an internal horn with front doors that opened and closed to control the volume.

The Antioch Baptist Church in St. Louis. It was built in 1920.

That day he learned a harsh lesson about following the rules. Still, his curiosity about music kept growing. He displayed an early talent for music. Berry sang in the choir when he was only six years old.

Martha and Henry Berry were the grandchildren of slaves. The Berry family was among the African Americans who migrated from the rural South to northern and Midwestern areas, like Chicago, Illinois, and St. Louis, Missouri. They were looking for employment during World War I. Henry Berry worked as a carpenter and served as a deacon of the Antioch Baptist Church. Martha Berry was one of the rare black women during this era to receive a college education. She worked as a teacher and school principal. Chuck's parents were hardworking and deeply religious. The Berry kids had a very strict upbringing.

Chuck was raised with three sisters and two brothers in a middle-class black neighborhood known as the Ville. The community housed many successful black-owned businesses and institutions. However, because he grew up in a segregated area, Berry was shocked the first time he saw white people in the neighborhood. He was three years old, and later recalled seeing white firemen fighting a blaze in a shed. Their skin color was so different from his that he thought their faces were white because they were afraid of the fire.[6] He didn't understand until his father explained it to him: "Daddy told me they were white people, and their skin was always white that way, day or night."[7]

In 1880, businessman Emile Berliner invented a flat phonograph record and a recording/playback device called the Gramophone. It was based on the cylinder phonograph introduced by Thomas Edison in 1877. But unlike Edison's device, it produced disk-shaped copies like a printing press. Berliner later asked engineer Eldridge Johnson, the owner of a machine shop in Camden, New Jersey, to help him develop a spring-wound motor to power the turntable on his new disk phonograph.

In 1905, Johnson founded The Victor Talking Machine Company. By this time he had made innovative changes to the recording machine. He tapered its tonearm, improved the sound box, and created a quieter motor that did not require it to be cranked by hand. He added a lid that a person could open to change the record or spear-shaped needle. The early machines displayed a huge bell-shaped horn on top of the box to amplify the sound. Many people hated the way it looked. Johnson built more attractive custom-painted cabinets and placed the horn inside. The design was patented and named Victrola.

Johnson lowered the cost once he built smaller portable machines. He paid opera stars and famous musicians to endorse his Victrolas. Sales increased tremendously. When radio was introduced, it offered better sound quality and more programs for listeners (music, news, and stories). Radio parts were added to the machine by the late 1920s. In 1929, Johnson sold the business to what became RCA Victor.

RCA's logo featured Nippy the dog listening to a Gramophone bearing the Victrola name until the early 1970s.

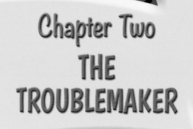

Chapter Two
THE TROUBLEMAKER

Rock's so good to me. Rock is my child and my grandfather.[1]

—*Chuck Berry*

Berry had many interests and hobbies growing up. He learned about carpentry from his father and worked with him on different building projects. His uncle, Harry Davis, a lover of science and a professional photographer, taught him the art of shooting and processing photographs. Berry gave serious thought to a career in photography. However, when he got older he attended night school to be a professional hairdresser.[2] Still, music turned out to be his greatest love.

His musical education bloomed as he learned how to play different instruments in school while singing in the church choir. He learned a great deal about classical music from his sister Lucy. Berry was able to quickly learn how to play all kinds of musical instruments, including the piano, bass, saxophone,

Chuck and his sister Lucy Ann in 1965. Berry had three sisters and two brothers.

Berry played Gibson guitars throughout his life. During his early years of success, he named one of his guitars after his first big hit: "Maybellene."

and drums. His favorite was the guitar, which he started playing in high school.

Berry attended Sumner High School in St. Louis. This prestigious institution was the first all-black school west of the Mississippi River. The students were mainly from wealthy professional and middle-class families, and the school boasted a strong tradition of classical music and opera.

In 1941, Chuck shocked the school when he played in a musical stage performance called the "All Men's Review." Accompanied by a friend playing guitar, he sang a blues song by Jay McShann called "Confessin' the Blues." The students in the auditorium raved over it and applauded loudly. The school faculty didn't. Teachers found it crude and disgusting. How dare this kid play a low-class blues song at their sophisticated school?

Chuck had no idea playing secular music would create such a problem. But that was okay. He was really excited that his performance proved to be such a big hit with the student body. His sudden popularity inspired him to pick up playing the guitar. He signed up for lessons and later studied with local jazz guitarist Ira Harris. Other more famous jazz and blues guitarists that had a major influence on him were Carl Hogan, T-Bone Walker, Charlie Christian, and Elmore James.

Aaron Thibeaux Walker (T-Bone Walker) inspired Berry to play the guitar behind his back, with his teeth, and while doing dance splits.

Count Basie, a Jazz composer, was the driving force behind boogie-woogie music.

Berry constantly listened to the radio. He was a big fan of boogie-woogie, big band music, swing, blues, and jazz. Another genre that appealed to him and strongly affected his future was country hillbilly music performed by white artists. Berry was able to weave country music and black rhythms into the music and lyrics of many of his songs. These new songs strongly appealed to both black and white audiences, a rarity at the time.

In high school, Berry sang and played guitar at parties. He developed into a terrific performer. Although a gifted musician, he did poorly in school. He had little interest in his studies. He rebelled against the school's decorum and strictness. He was considered a troublemaker.

In 1944, at the age of 17, Berry dropped out of high school. He decided to leave the Ville and run away from his family and his middle-class world with all those strict rules. On a whim he met up with two friends, Skip and James, and they set out to search for their fortunes in Hollywood, California. Driving in Berry's 1937 Oldsmobile, they were only 30 miles out of town when they ran headfirst into Jim Crow segregation. They stopped for food at a restaurant in Wentzville,

A young man drinks from a "Colored" water cooler in Oklahoma in 1939. Despite his success, Chuck Berry still faced Jim Crow segregation.

located in the all-white county of St. Charles. The boys were immediately ordered to go around to the back to receive their food from the kitchen.

Once the trio reached Kansas City, they had already run out of most of their money. By chance they found a handgun that was left in a parking lot. It didn't work, but they figured they could still scare people with it. They made the bad decision to go on a crime spree. They robbed a bakery, clothing store, and barbershop. When Berry's Oldsmobile broke down, they stole a car. The three young men were stopped outside of town by highway patrol and arrested. For nearly a month they were held in the Boone County Jail before being tried on the case. Even though they were minors and first-time offenders, they were sentenced to the maximum of 10 years in prison.[3]

**The Ohio State Reformatory (above) served as the model for the movie
The Shawshank Redemption. This and other reformatories were
detention centers for first time youth offenders.**

After his conviction, Berry was sent to the Intermediate Reformatory
for Young Men at Algoa, outside Jefferson City, Missouri. Inside the
reformatory, he spent time at the gym and trained to be a boxer. He
boxed briefly, but soon focused on his music again. He sang bass in a
gospel vocal quartet that he organized. It became very popular with
the inmates. Berry stated: "You ain't seen nothin' till you witness a
gang, who are supposed to be hostile, sitting there like apostles
hearing a soul-stirring gospel!"[4] The quartet was invited by a white
missionary, Mother Robinson, to sing for the services every Sunday at
the white dormitories. Soon, the authorities gave the group permission
to perform outside the correctional facility. In October 1947, after
serving three years, Berry was released due to good behavior. It was
his 21st birthday.

SUMNER HIGH SCHOOL

Sumner High School, in St. Louis, Missouri, was the first high school for African Americans west of the Mississippi River. It opened in 1875 with 411 students.[5] The school was named after Massachusetts Senator Charles Sumner, who was deeply committed to abolishing slavery and providing equality for African Americans. Sumner argued for the government to enlist more black soldiers during the Civil War. In 1848–1849, he helped to form the antislavery Free Soil Party and legally challenged Boston school segregation.

The Missouri Constitution adopted in 1865 required that regional school boards support the education of black students in their district.[6] This made it possible to establish Sumner High School. It remained the only high school for African Americans until 1927 when Vashon High School opened.

The school moved twice from its original location on 11th and Spruce. It has been at its current location on Cottage Street since 1908. The landmark school, whose building was designed by William B. Ittner, is on the National Register of Historic Places. Famous people who attended the school include Chuck Berry, tennis great Arthur Ashe (tennis legend), Ethel Hedgeman Lyle (founder of Alpha Kappa Alpha Sorority), Grace Bumbry (opera singer), Billy Davis (singer, The 5th Dimension), Dick Gregory (comedian), Robert Guillaume (actor, *Soap* and *Benson*), Wendell O. Pruitt (pioneering military pilot and Tuskegee Airman), and Tina Turner (Rock and Roll Hall of Fame singer).

Charles H. Sumner High School was the first public school for African Americans west of the Mississippi River.

Chapter Three
MARRIAGE, FAMILY, & HILLBILLY MUSIC

"Some of the clubgoers started whispering, 'Who is that black hillbilly at the Cosmo?' After they laughed at me a few times, they began requesting the hillbilly stuff and enjoyed trying to dance to it.[1]

—Chuck Berry

Once he was freed from jail, Berry returned to St. Louis. He worked long hours in his father's construction business with his brother Henry. Henry had just come back from serving in the army. He was now known as "Hank," a nickname his army pals gave him. In turn, he nicknamed his brother, Charles, "Chuck."[2] It caught on among family and friends. He started going by the name Chuck Berry.

Berry and a good buddy were strolling down a sidewalk when he spotted a striking-looking young woman enjoying an ice cream cone. To him, she looked like a "Polynesian princess."[3] He flirted with her and found out her name was Themetta Suggs. She worked in a dry-cleaning store. The two fell crazily in love. Months later, on October 28, 1948, they were married. He affectionately called her

Chuck Berry was like a new man once he was released in 1947 from the correctional facility. He worked every job he could to make money to improve his life. He soon met and fell in love with Themetta Suggs. They married and remained together for 68 years.

"Toddy." The couple would have four children: Ingrid, Melody, Aloha, and Charles Berry, Jr. Chuck and Toddy stayed married for the rest of his life.

Chuck supported his family by working as many jobs as he could. He briefly worked on the factory line at two automobile assembly plants. Chuck and Toddy lived in an apartment building rent-free because he took on a job as a custodian there. From time to time he worked as a part-time photographer for his uncle. Berry also trained as a beautician at the Poro College of Cosmetology. The school was founded by Annie Malone, who became a millionaire as a result of her hairdressing enterprise. Barbershops and beauty parlors were one of the most stable businesses in the black community and always had a steady flow of customers.

A barber shop in 1940 in the Negro Quarter of Durham, North Carolina. Styling hair was a great way to earn a living in the black community. Berry went to night school to learn hairdressing and cosmetology.

By 1950, Berry had earned enough money to buy a three-room brick house for $4,500. In this small house, he would create some of the greatest songs in rock and roll history. In 2008, the house was listed on the National Register of Historic Places.[4]

In this home at 3137 Whittier Street, Chuck Berry wrote most of his greatest hits.

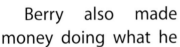

Berry also made money doing what he loved—playing music. In June 1952, Tommy Stevens, a former Sumner high school classmate, invited Berry to join his three-piece combo. The band had a regular gig at a sophisticated black nightclub called Huff's Garden in East St. Louis. The Tommy Stevens Combo played mainly blues and black pop standards. Berry brought something to the group they didn't have before: showmanship! The audience enjoyed his lively singing and guitar playing. One time Berry surprised the blues-loving audience. Out of nowhere he struck up a country-and-western tune.

Johnnie Johnson, a boogie-woogie pianist and local jazz celebrity, watched the act in the club that night. He couldn't forget the crowd's reaction: "The people seemed to really get a kick out of it. They'd be hollerin' and dancin' havin' a good ol' time!"[5]

Johnson was very impressed. He saw what an entertaining force Berry could be. Berry showed tons of charisma and could easily hold an audience. Dancing and playing to the crowd was the type of energy Johnson's band lacked. In 1952, his saxophone player got sick and wasn't going to be able to play for a New Year's Eve show. Johnson asked Berry to step in and play with his Sir John's Trio. He also wanted him to add some of those country tunes. He offered Berry the opportunity to make triple the amount of money to work in a larger club with a better band. Berry accepted his invitation. He played that night with the group in the Cosmopolitan, a popular black blues club in East St. Louis.

With Ebby Hardy, the drummer, banging out a country backbeat, Berry broke into a hillbilly song called "Mary Jo." The crowd went wild. Johnson said: "The people loved him. They just ate it up. . . . The public was always looking for something new, and a group of black men playing hillbilly songs was definitely new."[6]

The owner of Cosmopolitan saw Berry's value and insisted that Johnnie make him a permanent group member. It marked the beginning of a longtime collaboration between Berry and Johnson. Johnson's keyboard playing had a major influence on Berry's songs and guitar playing. Together they created an unusual but tremendously likeable sound.

Tommy Stevens called Berry in 1954 and offered him twice what he was making with the Sir John Trio to play with his former group at the Crank Club. In a blink, Berry was back with the Tommy Stevens Combo. He was also asked to play his guitar on a record with Calypso Joe. He loved the experience of writing songs and recording.

When the Cosmo owner begged him to come back and play with the Sir John Trio, he said he would under the following conditions: 1) He'd be bandleader. 2) He'd receive a contract. 3) The band could pursue record deals.[7]

The club owner agreed and Berry was back with the Sir John Trio. Berry's showmanship and the band's mix of jazz, rhythm and blues tunes, and country songs drew white patrons to the club. The trio became the hottest band in St. Louis.

Berry loved to experiment with musical ideas and often tested them out on people at the Cosmo. His popularity attracted a huge following of white youth eager to hear what he would play nightly. Berry's next goal was to record some of these novel ideas.

LET'S DO IT!

LET'S CRANK IT UP AT

THE CRANK CLUB

2742 Vanderventer, St. Louis, Mo.

CHUCK BERRYN

GUITAR AND COMBO

Richard Culph, Sax   Erskine Rodgers, Piano   Bill Erskine, Drums

DANCING AND ENTERTAINMENT

EVERY MONDAY, WEDNESDAY, FRIDAY & SATURDAY

EVERYONE WELCOME

Admission Free

A poster advertising one of Berry's first gigs. He added an "n" to his last name because he didn't want his father to be embarrassed by his secular music. He soon dropped the n.

ANNIE TURNBO MALONE

Businesswoman, chemist, inventor, and philanthropist Annie Turnbo Malone was one of the first black female millionaires in America.[8] She created and marketed hair care products for black women.

Annie Minerva Turnbo was born in Illinois on August 9, 1869, to Robert Turnbo and Isabella Cook. Her parents were former slaves. Her father fought in the Union Army during the Civil War. Annie's parents died when she was very young. Her older sister raised her. Annie was often ill. She didn't graduate from high school because she missed so many classes, but she was great at chemistry, and she was ambitious. She practiced hairdressing with her sister and decided she wanted to be a "beauty doctor."[9] She developed a chemical shampoo called The Great Wonderful Hair Grower. It could straighten black women's hair without damaging the hair or scalp like other products would. From there, she developed a line of hair care and beauty products.

In 1902, Turnbo moved her thriving business to St. Louis, which had the country's fourth-largest black population.[10] Black women were denied access to the mainstream markets, so she and her assistants sold her products by giving street demonstrations and selling door-to-door. One of her employees, Sarah Breedlove, left and started her own successful hair care business as Madame C.J. Walker.

Turnbo trademarked her revolutionary beauty products under the name Poro. She married Aaron Eugene Malone, a school principal in 1914. In 1918, she founded the first school of black cosmetology in America. It was built in the historic neighborhood of the Ville. The college employed over 175 people and set up shops and schools all over the world. The school's curriculum included training students on personal style and presentation. It graduated over 75,000 agents worldwide.

Malone was very generous, contributing thousands of dollars every year to educational programs, universities, YMCAs, and black orphanages. When she died in 1957, Poro beauty colleges existed in over 30 cities in the United States.

Berry attended Annie Turnbo Malone's Poro College in St. Louis. It became one of the most prestigious enterprises focused on African-American women's hair care, beauty, and cosmetics products in the world. By 1920, she was a multi millionaire.

Chapter Four
THE ETERNAL TEENAGER

"Chuck Berry was rock's greatest practitioner, guitarist, and the greatest pure rock & roll writer who ever lived."[1]

—*Bruce Springsteen*

In May 1955, Berry traveled to Chicago to pursue his fortune in a city famous for producing some of the hottest blues in the country. He attended the performance of his idol, legendary blues musician Muddy Waters, in a nightclub. Afterward, Berry asked Waters for advice on getting a recording contract. Waters suggested he see Leonard Chess, one of the founders of Chess Records. It was owned by brothers Leonard and Phil Chess.[2] Waters contacted Leonard Chess and raved about seeing Berry perform in St. Louis. Leonard wanted to meet Berry after catching the excitement in Muddy's voice.

Chess Records was a major blues label. Berry brought a blues demo tape to the audition. He and Johnnie Johnson had made the tape, called "Wee Wee Hours." It truly surprised him when the song they got excited about was Berry's version of the

Muddy Waters was called the "father of modern Chicago blues." He created such classic hits as "Got My Mojo Working" and "Hoochie Coochie Man." Waters introduced Berry to Leonard Chess of Chess Records, where he recorded his greatest songs.

Chess Records Studio in 2012. The company was founded in Chicago in 1950 and run by Leonard and Phil Chess. Recognized as one of the greatest rhythm and blues labels, it also expanded into country, soul, gospel and early rock and roll.

country song "Ida Red."[3] Chess' market had been shrinking, and the brothers were searching for music other than R&B.

A lighthearted fiddler's tune "Ida Red" was first recorded in 1950 by Bob Wills and the Texas Playboys. Berry changed the lyrics of the song to being about a car chase. In the story, the singer is in his car, chasing his girlfriend. She is speeding away in another car with another guy. Berry changed the title from "Ida Red" to "Maybellene." He had been trained as a cosmetologist, so he named it "Maybellene" after the popular cosmetics line. Berry, Johnson, drummer Ebby Hardy, bassist Willie Dixon, and Jerome Green (on maracas) headed into the studio on May 21 and cut the record. At one point, Berry sang in a bathroom to get an echo effect. It took 35 takes to get the song right. Phil Chess says, "It was different. . . . Like nothing we'd heard before. We figured if we could get that sound down on record we'd have a hit. . . . The song had a new kind of feel about it."[4] Berry quickly signed a contract.

Berry's vocals on "Maybellene," along with the combo of blues and country elements, exploded on the music charts. Alan Freed, a popular and influential white disc jockey, promoted blues, country, and rhythm and blues music. He called it rock and roll. Music scholars credit Freed for playing a major role in advancing rock and roll music as well as the rock concert business. He aired the single

Alan Freed promoted rarely played music to an international audience. He called it rock and roll. His live concerts featuring African-American music knocked down the walls of segregation, as black and white teenagers danced together.

"Maybellene" for two hours on his radio station WINS in New York. By September 10, 1955, the record had sold over one million copies and soared to No. 1 on *Billboard's* R&B chart and to No. 5 on the *Hot 100* pop chart.[5]

"Maybellene" was remarkable in another way. It was the first rock and roll song by a black artist to outsell its white cover version.[6] "The big beat, cars and young love . . . It was a trend, and we jumped on it," Leonard Chess remarked in an interview about the song's appeal.[7]

A bronze statue of Chuck Berry doing his duck walk. This one can be seen in Seattle. There are many similar statues across the United States.

"Wee Wee Hours" was placed on the B-side of the single "Maybellene." It rose to No. 10 on the *Billboard* R&B chart.

At an Alan Freed show at the Paramount Theater, Chuck Berry sang his hit "Maybellene." During his performance, for the first time outside of St. Louis and Chicago, Berry let loose with his crowd-pleasing "duck walk." It was one of his favorite guitar-playing stunts. He would crouch down on bent knees and walk across the stage, playing guitar and bobbing his head like a duck. It drove the crowd wild! Whenever he broke out with it, it was guaranteed to bring screams and applause. He basically owned that move. For decades to come, rock stars would mimic the duck walk or come up with their own versions.

At first, many radio listeners thought Chuck Berry was white. He was seen as a different type of R&B singer. His vocals were precise. He enunciated each word in a song. There wasn't that cool bluesy sound in his voice more common for blues singers of the era. Yet he could rock with the best of them. Teenagers loved him! He spoke to them in a way that hadn't been done before. He truly captured the spirit of the time.

Berry's most prized possession, his 1973 Cadillac El Dorado convertible, is a hot attraction in the National Museum of African American History & Culture in Washington, D.C.

His songs were about youth, having fun, dancing, romance, cars, and rebellion. Teenagers understood him and he seemed to understand them. And this was from a man who created his greatest hits while in his late twenties and early thirties. According to *Newsweek*, Berry's impact during rock's infancy made him "its first star guitarist and lyricist." His ability to meld blues, rockabilly, and jazz into timeless pop songs earned him the nickname, "the eternal teenager."[8]

Berry's songs were groundbreaking. His voice and the sassy twangs and riffs of his guitar were unlike any other. He made hit tunes for the next few years, producing one rock classic after another. After "Maybellene," he had a string of landmark songs, such as: "Roll Over, Beethoven," "Sweet Little Sixteen," "Johnny B. Goode," "Memphis,"

"School Day (Ring! Ring! Goes the Bell)," "Around and Around," "Brown-Eyed Handsome Man," "Rock and Roll Music," "Carol," "Guitar Boogie," and "Too Much Monkey Business." Berry with his storytelling ability accomplished crossover appeal with white teenagers without losing his black fans.

He once commented, "I made records for people who would buy them. . . . No color, no ethnic, no political—I don't want that, never did."[9] Berry was at the top of his game entering the 1960s. But trouble loomed once again in 1959.

Berry wrote and performed an incredible string of hits. This gifted musician merged country, rockabilly, swing, and rhythm and blues together to produce a sound that rose above the label "race records." It appealed to black and white audiences, a feat rarely achieved during this era.

CHESS RECORDS

Lejzor and Fiszel Czyz were Jewish brothers from Poland who immigrated to Chicago. When they arrived, their family Americanized their names to Leonard and Philip Chess. The brothers later opened a liquor store in an African American neighborhood in the South Side of Chicago. In 1946, they opened a nightclub called the Macomba Lounge.[10]

The club was a rough joint where shady folks and drug dealers hung out. But it was also known for having some of the best music they ever heard. Leonard Chess was determined to record some of this jazzy bebop, pop, and mellow blues ballads that were so popular in the club. He partnered with a small local label, Aristocrat Records, to do so. The first few records he produced bombed.

When Leonard listened to a Mississippi singer named Muddy Waters, he heard a rough country-sounding voice with a Delta growl. Waters sang "I Can't Be Satisfied" and backed it with a "whining electric slide guitar."[11] Leonard couldn't imagine anyone liking the song—until he was advised that black Southerners who were moving north for jobs might. He gambled and pressed 3,000 singles. They sold out in one day.

Stunned but impressed, Leonard wasted no time. He brought his brother on board. They renamed the company Chess Records. The Chess brothers went on to create one of the greatest musical catalogues in history. Sixty years later, that first recording by Muddy Waters was praised as the "masterpiece of electric Chicago blues."[12]

Chess Records released some of the most influential and innovative blues, R&B, and classic rock and roll tracks ever written. The music inspired a worldwide audience of listeners and musicians. When a 95-year-old Phil Chess was asked in 2016 why the duo were naturals to the blues, he answered: "We came from Poland in 1928. That was blues all the time."[13]

The Chess label

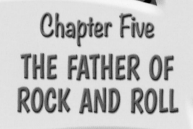

Chapter Five
THE FATHER OF ROCK AND ROLL

"Everything I wrote about wasn't about me, but about the people listening." [1]

—Chuck Berry

By the late 1950s, Berry was a major star. His touring schedule grew so hectic, he performed in 75 cities in 75 days. Berry was featured in Alan Freed's "The Biggest Show of Stars for 1957," sharing the stage with Buddy Holly, LaVern Baker, Fats Domino, Paul Anka, The Crickets, The Drifters, Jerry Lee Lewis, Frankie Lymon, The Everly Brothers, Clyde McPhatter, and Eddie Cochrane.[2]

Berry's live performances drew integrated crowds, and blacks and whites danced together. They also brought out the bigots who preferred that people remain segregated. Many parents feared this rock and roll music would turn their children into juvenile delinquents. They called it "immoral" and thought their kids would start acting and dressing like the rock artists they idolized.

Segregationists wanted to ban rock and roll. Asa Carter, leader of the White Citizens Council of

Chuck Berry, 1972. In that year, he scored his first number one song with the novelty tune "My Ding-a-Ling." He continued touring during the seventies and remained a popular concert draw.

Alabama, declared, "Rock and roll music is the basic, heavy-beat music of Negroes. It appeals to the base in man, brings out animalism and vulgarity." He claimed that rock and roll, and all "Negro music," was "designed to force Negro culture on the South."[3]

His opinion didn't change the music. Teenagers of all colors welcomed artists like Chuck Berry with open arms.

Berry appeared on TV shows such as *American Bandstand*. He was seen in the movies *Rock Rock Rock*, *Mister Rock and Roll*, and *Go, Johnny, Go!* In 1958, he performed at Rhode Island's Newport Jazz Festival. The concert was released as the documentary *Jazz on a Summer's Day*. Berry performed alongside such jazz giants as Thelonious Monk, Max Roach, Louis Armstrong, and Dinah Washington. Keith Richards of the Rolling Stones fondly remembers Chuck Berry playing "Sweet Little Sixteen": "When I saw Chuck in *Jazz on a Summer's Day* as a teenager, what struck me was how he was playing against the grain with a bunch of jazz guys . . . they were brilliant . . . but they had that jazz attitude cats put on sometimes. . . . Chuck took them all by storm. . . . To me, that's blues. That's the attitude and the guts it takes. That's what I wanted to be."[4]

Chuck Berry received a **PEN** Award for songwriting excellence at the John F. Kennedy Presidential Library and Museum in Boston. Keith Richards showed up to play his own Gibson guitar to pay tribute to Berry.

Berry was very business-minded. He wasn't afraid to stand up for his rights as a musical artist. He demanded to be paid in cash for his performances. He purchased 30 acres of land in Wentzville, Missouri, in 1957. There he built an amusement park called Berry Park, which opened to the public in 1961. In 1958, he opened a nightclub called Club Bandstand in downtown St. Louis. The racially integrated club hosted a band every night, with floor shows on the weekends.[5]

In 1959, Berry was traveling in Mexico and met Janice Escalanti. He brought her back to the United States to work as a hatcheck girl at his nightclub. Weeks later he fired her. It turned out she was under 21 and Berry was arrested for bringing one so young across state lines. His first conviction was overturned because the judge repeatedly used racial slurs.[7] When the case went back to court, Berry was again found guilty. He served 20 months in federal prison in Indiana.

Friends noticed that Berry was not the same man after his release in 1963. Carl Perkins, a rockabilly singer-guitarist whose most famous song was "Blue Suede Shoes," recalls touring Britain with Berry in 1964: "Never saw a man so changed. He had been an easygoing guy before, the kinda guy who'd jam in dressing rooms, sit and swap guitar licks and jokes. In England he was cold, real distant and bitter."[8]

Berry continued to write and perform music. During the 1960s his hits included "Nadine,"

Carl Lee Perkins, called "the King of Rockabilly" was a good friend of Berry's. His songs include "Blue Suede Shoes," "Matchbox," and "Honey Don't." They were recorded by the Beatles, Elvis Presley, and Jimi Hendrix.

Chuck Berry in 1971. Berry continued to tour and write songs.

"You Can Never Tell," Promised Land," "Dear Dad," and "No Particular Place to Go." He discovered his music had reached a new generation. Young rock bands not only covered his songs but were changing the music and culture. He was admired by the Beatles, Rolling Stones, Beach Boys, Yardbirds, and so many more. Berry sued and won a lawsuit against the Beach Boys, whose "Surfin' U.S.A." was a reworked version of "Sweet Little Sixteen."[9]

Berry continued to tour, often playing with bands that grew up on his music. In 1972, he scored the biggest hit of his career with the novelty song "My Ding-a-Ling." The song was a million-seller and his only No. 1 pop single. In 1979, he performed for President Jimmy Carter at the White House. The Grammy Recording Academy recognized Berry as a rock pioneer, presenting him with a lifetime achievement award in 1984. That same year, director Taylor Hackford filmed him at his home in Wentzville for the documentary *Hail! Hail! Rock 'n' Roll*. It featured performances by Berry with a band led by Keith Richards of the Rolling Stones. When the Rock and Roll Hall of Fame and Museum opened in in 1995, Berry performed at the inaugural concert, backed by Bruce Springsteen and the E Street Band.[10]

The "Father of Rock 'n' Roll," Chuck Berry died on March 18, 2017. Among his numerous honors, a statue was dedicated to him in St. Louis immortalizing his duck walk. He received a PEN, New England's inaugural award for Song Lyrics of Literary Excellence, and in 2000 he was given the Kennedy Center Honors Award. President Bill Clinton praised him as "one of the twentieth century's most influential musicians. He also thanked him for "making us laugh, making us dance and making us happy."[11]

One of the most fitting tributes for Chuck Berry's legacy is that his recording of "Johnny B. Goode" is the only rock song on the *Sounds of Earth* gold record, which was launched into space aboard the two Voyager spacecraft in 1977. A spokesperson for the Jet Propulsion Lab remarked: "Johnny B. Goode will be rock and roll's representative to the universe."[12]

In 2012, the Rock and Roll Hall of Fame honored the rock and roll trailblazer with its American Music Masters Series. It was titled *Roll Over Beethoven: The Life and Music of Chuck Berry*. It featured a week of panel discussions, interviews, films, and other programs. Berry performed to close out the event.

THE ROCK AND ROLL HALL OF FAME

The Rock and Roll Hall of Fame Museum in Cleveland, Ohio, first opened its doors on September 2, 1995. The building was designed by the world-famous Chinese-American architect, I.M. Pei. A number of cities such as New York, San Francisco, Memphis, and Chicago competed for the museum to be established in their area. Cleveland won the competition with over 600,000 signatures from their fan base and a $65 million commitment from the city. Cleveland also served as the home of Alan Freed, the beloved radio disc jockey largely credited for inventing the term *rock and roll*. In order to create the museum, the Rock and Roll Foundation was formed in 1983.[13]

The museum was established to honor all areas of rock and roll. Inductees fall into four categories: Performers, Non-performers, Early Influences, and Side-men. Performers are not eligible until 25 years after their first album is released. The first inductees into the Hall of Fame were Chuck Berry, James Brown, Ray Charles, Fats Domino, the Everly Brothers, Buddy Holly, Jerry Lee Lewis, and Elvis Presley.

The grand opening in 1995 was celebrated with a spectacular benefit concert at the Cleveland Municipal Stadium. Chuck Berry performed with Bruce Springsteen & The E Street Band. Other greats performed as well, including James Brown, Bob Dylan, Jerry Lee Lewis, Aretha Franklin, Johnny Cash, and Booker T. and the MGs. Opening weekend also included a parade in downtown Cleveland and an appearance by Little Richard and Yoko Ono.

The Rock and Roll Hall of Fame was built to honor the most popular and influential people who have shaped rock and roll.

1926 Charles Edward Anderson Berry is born in St. Louis, Missouri, on October 18.

1932 Blues pianist and composer Thomas A. Dorsey writes "Take My Hand, Precious Lord."

1941 The United States enters World War II after Japan attacks Pearl Harbor on December 8. The U.S. Army creates the Tuskegee Air Squadron, the first African Americans to serve as pilots.

1947 Chuck Berry is released from Algoa Reformatory after serving 3 years of a 10-year sentence for armed robbery.

1948 Berry marries Themetta "Toddy" Suggs, with whom he will have four children.

1949 The term *rhythm and blues* is first used by Jerry Wexler of *Billboard* magazine. It replaces the old term of "race" records.

1952 Pianist and bandleader Johnnie Johnson asks Berry to stand in for his ailing saxophonist for a New Year's Show. Berry joins his trio.

1953 *Go Tell It on the Mountain*, the first novel by James Baldwin, is published.

1954 The Supreme Court rules in favor of school desegregation in *Brown v. Board of Education*.

1955 Berry meets his idol, Muddy Waters. He signs a contract with Chess Records. He records "Maybellene," which is a rewrite of the country song "Ida Red." "Maybellene" sells over one million copies and reaches number one on the *Billboard* rhythm and blues chart.

1956 Berry's "Roll Over, Beethoven" rises to No. 2 on the R&B chart and No. 29 on the pop chart. Nat King Cole is attacked on stage during a segregated performance in Alabama.

1957 Berry's first album, *After School Session*, is released. The single "School Day" reaches No. 3 on pop charts and tops the R&B chart. Berry buys 30 acres of farmland outside Wentzville, Missouri.

1958 Berry's rock classic "Johnny B. Goode" (inspired by Johnnie Johnson) is released and makes the top ten. "Sweet Little Sixteen" reaches No 2 on the pop chart and tops the R&B chart. Berry's Club Bandstand opens.

1961 Berry Park in Wentzville, Missouri, opens to the public.

1962 Berry is convicted and sentenced in January to three years in prison for transporting an underage girl across state lines.

1963   Berry is released from prison on his 37th birthday. He discovers there is a new generation of artists influenced by him and playing his songs, such as the Rolling Stones, the Beatles, and the Beach Boys. At the March on Washington, Mahalia Jackson sings and Martin Luther King, Jr. delivers his "I Have a Dream" speech.

1964   Berry releases hit songs like "No Particular Place to Go," "You Never Can Tell," and "Nadine."

1966   Berry signs with Mercury Records.

1967   A compilation of Chuck Berry's classic hits, *Golden Decade,* is released by Chess Records.

1970   Berry re-signs with Chess Records. He is in high demand for concert tours.

1972   Berry's novelty single "My Ding-A-Ling" is his first and only No. 1 pop hit. The album it is on, *The London Chuck Berry Sessions,* reaches No. 8.

1977   Two Voyager spacecraft are launched with Berry's golden record "Johnny B. Goode" on it.

1979   Berry performs at the White House at the request of President Jimmy Carter. Months later he serves several months in prison for tax evasion.

1984   Berry is honored with the Grammy Lifetime Achievement Award.

1986   Berry is inducted into the Rock & Roll Hall of Fame.

1987   *Hail! Hail! Rock 'n' Roll*, a documentary of Berry's Fox Theatre Concert in St. Louis, is released to celebrate Berry's 60th Birthday.

1996   Berry begins monthly performances at Blueberry Hill's Duck Room in St. Louis.

2000   He receives Kennedy Center Honors.

2012   The Rock and Roll Hall of Fame honors him with its American Music Masters Series.

2016   On his 90th birthday, Berry announces plans to release his first album since 1979, called *Chuck*, sometime in 2017.

2017   Chuck Berry dies on March 18 at his home in St. Louis. His twentieth and final album was released on June 16. The album is favorably reviewed by critics. One of the 10 songs is a sequel to his classic "Johnny B. Goode", called "Lady B. Goode."

Chapter 1: Musical Roots

1. Sarah Larson, "Chuck Berry at Ninety: Full Speed Ahead," *The New Yorker*, October 18, 2016. https://www.newyorker.com/culture/sarah-larson/chuck-berry-at-ninety-full-speed-ahead

2. Chuck Berry, *Chuck Berry: The Autobiography* (New York: Harmony Books, 1987), p. 1.

3. Ibid., p. 3.

4. Ibid., p. 3.

5. Ibid., p. 4.

6. Bruce Pegg, *Brown Eyed Handsome Man: The Life and Hard Times of Chuck Berry* (New York: Routledge, 2002), p. 10.

7. "Chuck Berry: Songwriter, Singer, Guitarist (1926–2017)," *Biography*, https://www.biography.com/people/chuck-berry-9210488.

Chapter 2: The Troublemaker

1. Ralph Ellis, Todd Leopold, and Tony Marco, "Chuck Berry, Rock 'n' Roll Pioneer, Dead at 90," CNN, March 18, 2017. https://www.cnn.com/2017/03/18/entertainment/chuck-berry-dies/index.html.

2. Charles River Editors, *American Legends: The Life of Chuck Berry* (Cambridge: Createspace Independent Publishing Platform, 2014), "Chapter 1: Early Years."

3. "Chuck Berry: Songwriter, Singer, Guitarist (1926–2017)," *Biography*, https://www.biography.com/people/chuck-berry-9210488

4. *Chuck Berry: The Autobiography*, p. 61.

5. Sumner High School, "(Structures) Mound City on the Mississippi: A St. Louis History," http://dynamic.stlouis-mo.gov/history/structdetail.cfm?Master_ID=1638.

6. "Sumner High School," *CLIO*, https://www.theclio.com/web/entry?id=13412.

Chapter 3: Marriage, Family, & Hillbilly Music

1. Tim Brookes, *Guitar: An American Life*, (New York: Grove Press, 2005), p. 177.

2. Chuck Berry, *Chuck Berry: The Autobiography* (New York: Harmony Books, 1987), p. 74.

3. Bruce Pegg, *Brown Eyed Handsome Man: The Life and Hard Times of Chuck Berry* (New York: Routledge, 2002), p. 20.

4. Greg Bailey, "Around and Around: St. Louis Community Hopes to Restore Chuck Berry's House," *National Trust for Historic Preservation*, https://savingplaces.org/stories/around-and-around-st-louis-community-restore-chuck-berry-house#.Wqgm5pMbM3g

5. Pegg, p. 25.

6. Ibid., pp. 25, 26.

7. Ed Ward, *The History of Rock & Roll: Volume One 1920-1963* (New York: Flatiron Books, 2016), pp. 90–91.

8. "Annie Malone: A Generous Entrepreneur," The Freeman Institute, http://www.freemaninstitute.com/poro.htm.

9. "Malone, Annie Turnbo (1869–1957)," *Blackpast.org*, http://www.blackpast.org/aah/annie-turnbo-malone-1869-1957

10. "Annie Malone: A Generous Entrepreneur."

Chapter 4: The Eternal Teenager

1. "Chuck Berry, Rock & Roll Innovator, Dead at 90," *Rolling Stone*, March 18, 2017. https://www.rollingstone.com/music/news/chuck-berry-rock-roll-innovator-dead-at-90

2. Ed Ward, *The History of Rock & Roll: Volume One 1920-1963* (New York: Flatiron Books, 2016), p. 101.

3. "Chuck Berry," https://www.history-of-rock.com/berry.htm.

4. Ward, p. 103.

5. "Chuck Berry," https://www.history-of-rock.com/berry.htm.

6. Bruce Pegg, *Brown Eyed Handsome Man: The Life and Hard Times of Chuck Berry* (New York: Routledge, 2002), p. 42.

7. Jon Pareles, "Chuck Berry, Rock 'n' Roll Pioneer, Dies at 90." *The New York Times*, March 18, 2017. https://www.nytimes.com/2017/03/18/arts/chuck-berry-dead.html.

8. "Rock Legend Chuck Berry, the Eternal Teenager, Dies at 90," *Newsweek*, March 18, 2017. http://www.newsweek.com/rock-legend-chuck-berry-dies-90-570595

9. "Chuck Berry: Songwriter, Singer, Guitarist (1926–2017)," *Biography*, https://www.biography.com/people/chuck-berry-9210488

10. "Chess Records: How Two Polish Brothers Made Music History," *Culture.pl*, http://culture.pl/en/article/chess-records-how-two-polish-brothers-made-music-history.

11. Elijah Wald, "How the Blues Brothers behind Chess Records Made All the Right Moves," *The Guardian*, November 6, 2010. https://www.theguardian.com/music/2010/nov/06/leonard-phil-marshall-chess-records.

12. Ibid.

13. "Chess Records: How Two Polish Brothers Made Music History."

Chapter 5: The Father of Rock and Roll

1. Ralph Ellis, Todd Leopold, and Tony Marco, "Chuck Berry, Rock 'n' Roll Pioneer, Dead at 90," *CNN*, March 18, 2017. https://www.cnn.com/2017/03/18/entertainment/chuck-berry-dies/index.html.

2. "Moondog Alan Freed," The Pop History Dig, n.d. http://www.pophistorydig.com/topics/tag/alan-freed-stage-shows/

3. "Rock 'n' Roll in the Press," quoting "White Council vs. Rock and Roll," *Time*, April 18, 1956. http://www.umsl.edu/virtualstl/phase2/1950/events/perspectives/documents/rocknroll.html

4. Patrick Doyle, "Flashback: Chuck Berry Performs at 1958 Newport Jazz Festival," *Rolling Stone*, March 18, 2017. https://www.rollingstone.com/music/videos/see-chuck-berry-perform-at-1958-newport-jazz-festival-w472742.

5. Chuck Berry, *Chuck Berry: The Autobiography* (New York: Harmony Books, 1987), pp. 170–172.

6. Ed Ward, *The History of Rock & Roll: Volume One 1920-1963* (New York: Flatiron Books, 2016), pp. 218–219.

7. "Chuck Berry, Rock & Roll Innovator, Dead at 90," *Rolling Stone*, https://www.rollingstone.com/music/news/chuck-berry-rock-roll-innovator-dead-at-90.

8. Pegg, *Brown Eyed Handsome Man: The Life and Hard Times of Chuck Berry* (New York: Routledge, 2002), p. 171.

9. Ellis, Leopold, and Marco.

10. Jon Pareles, "Chuck Berry, Rock 'n' Roll Pioneer, Dies at 90." *The New York Times*, March 18, 2017. https://www.nytimes.com/2017/03/18/arts/chuck-berry-dead.html

11. "Chuck Berry among 2000 Kennedy Center Honorees," *Jet*, December 18, 2000, Vol. 99, No. 2.

12. "Chuck Berry Biography," *The John F. Kennedy Center for the Performing Arts*, http://www.kennedy-center.org/Artist/A3699

13. "Rock and Roll Hall of Fame Museum," *Ohio History Central*, http://www.ohiohistorycentral.org/w/Rock_and_Roll_Hall_of_Fame_Museum.

Works Consulted

Berry, Chuck. *Chuck Berry: The Autobiography*. New York: Harmony Books, 1987.

Charles River Editors. *American Legends: The Life of Chuck Berry*. Cambridge: Createspace Independent Publishing Platform, 2014.

Cohodas, Nadine. *Spinning Blues into Gold: The Chess Brothers and the Legendary Chess Records*. New York: St. Martin's Press, 2001.

"History of the Victor Phonograph," *The Victor-Victrola Page*, http://www.victor-victrola. com/History%20of%20the%20Victor%20Phonograph.htm

Pegg, Bruce. *Brown Eyed Handsome Man: The Life and Hard Times of Chuck Berry*. New York: Routledge, 2002.

Ward, Ed. *The History of Rock & Roll: Volume One 1920–1963*. New York: Flatiron Books, 2016.

Books

Buckland, Gail, *Who Shot Rock & Roll: A Photographic History, 1955 to the Present*. New York: Alfred A. Knopf, 2009.

Covach, John, and Andrew Flory. *What's That Sound? An Introduction to Rock and Its History*. New York: W.W. Norton & Co., 2012.

Kallen, Stuart, A. *The History of Rock and Roll (The Music Library)*. New York: Lucent Books, 2012.

Mahin, Michael. *Muddy: The Story of Blues Legend Muddy Waters*. New York: Atheneum Books, 20017.

Robertson, Robbie. *Legends, Icons & Rebels: Music That Changed the World*. Toronto: Tundra Books, 2013.

On the Internet

"Chuck Berry: His Colorful Life in Pictures." BBC, n.d. http://www.bbc.com/news/entertainment-arts-39318871

Daniel S. Levine, "Chuck Berry's Children: 5 Fast Fact You Need To Know," *Heavy*, March 2017. https://heavy.com/entertainment/2017/03/chuck-berry-children-biography-family-kids-dead-charles-aloha-melody-age-son-daughters/

Jayson Reynolds, "Chuck Berry's Wife & Children Are a Testament to His Lasting Love," *Inquisitr*, March 19, 2017. https://www.inquisitr.com/4070956/chuck-berrys-wife-children-are-a-testament-to-his-lasting-love/

"Six Facts about Chuck Berry." ENCA, n.d. https://www.enca.com/life/six-facts-about-chuck-berry.

ambitious (am-BIH-shus)—Having a strong desire to be successful.

amplify (AM-plih-fy)—To make louder.

autobiography (aw-toe-by-AH-gruh-fee)—A story a person writes about his or her own life.

charisma (kuh-RIZ-muh)—Charm and appeal.

conviction (kun-VIK-shun)—A court decision that a person is wrong or guilty of a crime..

decorum (day-KOR-um)—Respectful and polite behavior.

enunciate (ee-NUN-see-ayt)—To clearly pronounce a word or words.

floor show—A series of performances, such as singing, dancing, and comedy acts, performed at a nightclub.

harmony (HAR-muh-nee)—Notes sung or played at the same time to produce a pleasing sound.

inaugural (in-AW-gyuh-rul)—Marking a beginning, especially when it involves someone taking office for the first time.

infantile (IN-fin-tyl)—Childish, silly, annoying, or impolite.

influence (IN-floo-ents)—To change or affect someone naturally.

innovative (IN-noh-vay-tiv)—New, unique, and creative.

inspire (in-SPYR)—To make someone want to do or create something.

legendary (LEH-jen-dayr-ee)—Very well known for a long time.

logo (LOH-goh)—A symbol that identifies a company and appears on its products.

patron (PAY-trun)—Someone who gives to a business or organization.

philanthropist (fih-LAN-thruh-pist)—A person who donates or gives money to people or organizations to better other people's lives.

posthumous (PAH-styoo-mus)—Occurring after a person's death.

prestigious (preh-STIH-jus)—Having respect or admiration.

reformatory (reh-FOR-muh-tor-ee)—A type of jail where young or first offenders are sent for schooling or training.

secular (SEH-kyoo-lur)—Not spiritual or religious.

segregate (SEH-greh-gayt)—To separate, especially according to race.

symphony (SYM-fuh-nee)—A complex musical piece written for many instruments.